STUFFING CHRISTMAS

Warren Lane

dizzyemupublishing.com

DIZZY EMU PUBLISHING

1714 N McCadden Place, Hollywood, Los Angeles 90028

dizzyemupublishing.com

Stuffing Christmas
Warren Lane

First published in the United States
in 2022 by Dizzy Emu Publishing

dizzyemupublishing.com

STUFFING CHRISTMAS

Warren Lane

FADE IN:

EXT. HIGHWAY - A RAINY DAY

Lizzy's CAR moves down a grey rainy highway.

INT. LIZZY'S MOVING CAR - SAME

The windshield wipers slosh water aside to reveal LIZZY (35)
behind the wheel, a put-together Caucasian. Beside her,
riding shotgun is DAVE-O (35), a disheveled Caucasian.

                    DAVE-O
               (Australian accent)
          Thanksgiving is what exactly?

                    LIZZY
               (American Southern accent)
          It's when we made good with the
          Indigenous People way back when.

                    DAVE-O
          Didn't you destroy them and their
          culture? The Indigenous People.

                    LIZZY
          Yes, but--

                    DAVE-O
          Thanksgiving can get stuffed!

                    LIZZY
          Thanksgiving can get stuffed?

                    DAVE-O
          It's celebrating colonizers
          befriending the Indigenous People!
          Thanksgiving is a bollocks holiday!

                    LIZZY
          Yes, but now Thanksgiving is all
          about family 'n over-eating,
          there'll be heaps of turkey. Heaps.

                    DAVE-O
          Wait, ya mean, I can finally make
          my dream come true? Just like in
          all the American holiday movies?

                    LIZZY
          Yup, you're finally gonna get your
          very own heaping plate of turkey
          covered in glistening gravy.

                    DAVE-O
          Beauty, babes!

INT. ROBERT'S MOVING SUV - SAME

The windshield wipers slosh water aside to reveal Robert (40)
behind the wheel. He is Caucasian and in a *"Turkey Time!"*
sweater. Beside him, JEANNETTE (37), African American and
sporting little feathery turkey earrings, rides shotgun.

                    ROBERT
               (American Southern accent)
          Bobby, we can play football after
          Thanksgiving dinner, son.

                    JEANETTE
               (American Southern accent)
          After Thanksgiving dinner, son.

Jeanette turns, looking to the backseat where BOBBY (10), a
multiracial kid, and JENNY (13), a multiracial teenager, sit.

                    BOBBY
               (American Southern accent)
          Fabtastic.

                    ROBERT
          Why do you wanna play football
          anyhow? You hate football, there's
          no football on *Rupaul's Drag Race*.

                    JENNY
               (American Southern accent)
          Dad, I still have to pee.

                    ROBERT
          Hold it we're almost there.

                    JENNY
               (exploding)
          Stop gaslighting me!

                    ROBERT
               (matching her explosion)
          I'm not, we're really almost there!

Robert's face grows red as Jeanette calmly rubs his arm.

                    JEANETTE
          Breathe, honey, you don't wanna
          have one of your panic attacks.

EXT. BONNIE & STEVE'S HOUSE - SAME MOMENT BUT SUNNY HERE

Sun shines onto a MAILBOX: *"WALTON."* Fresh rainwater drips
from the box. Reveal that the mailbox stands at the end of a
driveway which leads to a HOUSE. Behind it is woods and a
barn. In the front yard a tree with a RING-SWING stands.

INT. BONNIE & STEVE'S HOUSE - KITCHEN - SAME

BONNIE (66), Caucasian and the quintessential grandmother
type, pulls a stuffed browned turkey out from her oven. She
rests the turkey atop the stove. CRACK--she looks to the
KITCHEN TABLE. Sitting at the table, CRACKING nuts, is STEVE
(66), also Caucasian and the quintessential grandfather type.

                    STEVE
               (American Southern accent)
          Is the turkey ready, dear?

                    BONNIE
               (American Southern accent)
          Yes, no thanks to you, *dear*!

                    STEVE
               (exploding)
          No bickering! We promised the kids!

ALVIN, an old golden retriever, at his feet BARKS.

                    STEVE
               (calmly to Alvin)
          That's right, boy, no bickering.
               (to Bonnie)
          Ready to tell 'em about the farm?

                    BONNIE
          No, why did you promise it to 'em?

                    STEVE
          Cuz I love this place 'n it's all I
          could offer 'em growing up.

                    BONNIE
               (shaking her head)
          Terrorists will gitcha every time.

                    STEVE
          You think our kids are terrorists?

                    BONNIE
          Yes 'n they're the worst kind.

                    STEVE
          What kind is that?

                    BONNIE
          The emotionally manipulative kind.

                    STEVE
          They didn't emotionally manipulate
          me into promising 'em the farm.

                    BONNIE
          They didn't?

                    STEVE
          No, they were just kids then. My
          promise just sorta slipped out one
          day when I was playing Verminator
          with Robert then it slipped out
          again another day when I was
          playing Troll Y'alls with Lizzy. I
          woulda promised 'em the world if I
          could but all I had was this place.
          I love this place 'n I love them.

                    BONNIE
          But if you love this place so much,
          why did you just sell it, dear?

                    STEVE
          Cuz I love you more, dear, I also
          made you a promise forty years ago.
          The only way you'd let me buy the
          farm is if I swore that one day I'd
          sell it so we could live out our
          golden years down in Florida, well,
          it's golden time. I already bought
          us the condo, it's a place called
          the Sunshine Towers, they clean
          your condo once a week.

Bonnie swoons, dramatically putting a hand to her forehead.

                    BONNIE
          Oh, Steve.

                    STEVE
          I love you too, dear.

Bonnie does a "sexy" dance over to Steve then kisses him.

                    BONNIE
Just tell the kids you sold the
farm, emotionally manipulative
terrorists they may be but they
know the rules, if you promised me
something first, I have dibs, dear.

                    STEVE
          (groaning)
Argh, this is gonna be the worst
Thanksgiving ever.

                    BONNIE
Tell everyone over dinner, the
sooner you tell 'em the better,
otherwise you'll worry all weekend.

                    STEVE
Okay, I'll come clean about the
farm if we can tell 'em a teeny-
tiny white lie alongside it.

                    BONNIE
What?

                    STEVE
That we're divorcing.

                    BONNIE
          (exploding)
No, I will not have another visit
ruined by one of your whoppers!

                    STEVE
But I can't look into their sweet-
sweet faces 'n tell 'em I sold the
farm without having one of my
whoppers to distract 'em, I can't
watch 'em realize that their dear
old Dad is a promise-liar.

                    BONNIE
They already know you're a promise-
liar, you've broken promises to 'em
thousands of times 'n they still
love you for some reason. Besides I
have dibs, dear, dems da rules.

                    STEVE
          (exploding)
Come on, dear, they don't adhere to
our rules anymore 'n I think this
promise-lie will be the one!

                    BONNIE
The one? Whataya mean?

                    STEVE
This is my biggest baddest promise-
lie yet. Selling the family farm
when I promised it to both of them?

                    BONNIE
It is pretty bad.

                    STEVE
So bad they'll finally disown us,
we'll never see the grands again.
          (he calms)
Look, I'll come clean about the
farm if you first announce we're
divorcing, they'll only believe our
"divorce" if it comes from you,
I've told too many whoppers.

                    BONNIE
You think telling this divorce-
whopper will distract 'em from the
truth so much that they'll be too
shocked to get "disowning-us-mad."

                    STEVE
Yup, we'll still get to see the
grands 'til we're dead like we
planned. Clever, huh, dear?

                    BONNIE
Yes, dear, very clever, only thing
is we'll have to keep up the facade
of our "divorce" all weekend.

                    STEVE
No, we won't.

                    BONNIE
We won't?

                    STEVE
No cuz right after our "divorce
announcement" we'll get "back
together" for the "good of the
family."

                    BONNIE
But when they ask about it later,
why do we say we sold the farm?

                    STEVE
          It was a decision made under
          "divorce-fueled-passion."

                    BONNIE
               (nodding)
          Makes sense.

                    STEVE
               (getting excited)
          Tell me we're getting a "divorce,"
          try it out for practice, dear.

                    BONNIE
          "We're getting a divorce," dear.

                    STEVE
          Nice but don't say, "dear." It'll
          make 'em savvy to our whopper.

                    BONNIE
          What about the grands?

                    STEVE
          What about 'em?

                    BONNIE
          I can't tell 'em we're getting a
          "divorce." That's messed up.

                    STEVE
          You can do it, dear.

                    BONNIE
               (exploding)
          No, I can't, *dear*!

                    ROBERT (O.S.)
          No bickering on Thanksgiving!

Robert jumps into the KITCHEN from around a WOODEN CORNER.

                    ROBERT
          Y'all promised, no bickering! The
          door was unlocked so we came in.

Alvin wags his tail, going to Robert who bends down.

                    ROBERT
          Alvin!

Alvin licks his face.

                    ROBERT
          I missed you too, boy!
              (doggy talk)
          I did, yes, I did!

Robert pops to and excitedly hugs Bonnie.

                    ROBERT
      Mom!

Robert looks to Steve.

                    ROBERT
      Dad!

He excitedly hugs Steve.

                    ROBERT
          Whataya been doin', old man?

Robert looks to the table, spying several nut shells atop it.

                    ROBERT
              (shaking his head)
          Eating nuts, not helping, some
          things never change.

                    BONNIE
          That's all your father did while I
          prepared everything, he's useless.

                    ROBERT
              (exploding)
          No bickering, Mom!

                    STEVE
          We're not bickering, Rob, we're
          fighting cuz your mother 'n I are
          getting a...the grands aren't here
          so you tell him, Bonnie.

                    BONNIE
          Okay, Rob, we're getting a--

                    JEANETTE (O.S.)
          Hey, Mom 'n Dad!

Jeanette jumps into the kitchen also from around the wooden
corner. She excitedly hugs Bonnie and Steve at the same time.

                    JEANETTE
          So good to see you 'n be offa that
          road! Bobby is out front swinging
          'n Jenny is using your bathroom!

                    JENNY (O.S.)
          No, I'm done, Mom.

Jenny jumps into the kitchen from around the wooden corner.

                    BONNIE
          My number one grand!

                    JENNY
          Mamaw!

Bonnie and Jenny excitedly hug.

                    ROBERT
          What were you saying, Mom, you're
          "getting a" what exactly?

                    BONNIE
               (still hugging Jenny)
          It's not important, we'll talk
          about it when Lizzy's here. Where
          is your sister anyhow, Rob?

                    ROBERT
          Probably still on the road.

EXT. A COUNTRY ROAD - SAME MOMENT

Lizzy's car barrels down a sloppily paved country road.

INT. LIZZY'S CAR - SAME

Lizzy still drives while Dave-O still rides shotgun.

                    LIZZY
          We're almost there, I hope you love
          the farm cuz I'm gonna own the
          place someday. My Dad promised.

                    DAVE-O
          When do you think you'll own it?

                    LIZZY
          By the time you 'n I are married.

                    DAVE-O
          Married? No, thanks. Gutted?

Lizzy smacks Dave-O on the shoulder, he mischievously smiles.

                    DAVE-O
          I'm just kidding, babes, don't
          worry, I'll marry you someday.

                    LIZZY
          You better.

Lizzy slows and pulls the car onto

THE DRIVEWAY OF BONNIE & STEVE'S HOUSE - SAME

Lizzy's car drives down the driveway and stops behind
Robert's parked SUV. In the front yard, from the single tree,
Bobby swings on the ring, Alvin wags his tail below him.

                                        BACK TO:

INT. LIZZY'S PARKED CAR - SAME

Lizzy, behind the wheel, and Dave-O, passenger, sit. They
stare at Bobby, ring-swinging, and Alvin, wagging his tail.

                    DAVE-O
          Eat your heart out Disney Plus.

                    LIZZY
          That's Bobby, he's Rob 'n
          Jeanette's kid. Bobby 'n I watch
          Rupaul's Drag Race religiously 'n I
          wanna eat him up with a side of
          ketchup, he's that cute.

Dave-O opens his passenger door.

                    DAVE-O
          Hey, Bobby, I'm Dave-O!

Dave-O steps out. Bobby jumps down from the ring-swing.

EXT. BONNIE & STEVE'S DRIVEWAY - SAME

Lizzy steps out of her PARKED CAR. She closes her door,
staring at Robert's parked SUV in front of her.

                    LIZZY
                (to herself)
          Rob, when did you get this?

                    FATIMA (O.S.)
          Happy Thanksgiving, Lizzy!

Lizzy looks to

FATIMA & MUHAMMAD'S HOUSE - SAME

This is the only HOUSE nearby, in the yard is a tall PINE
TREE. MUHAMMAD (75), Arab American, wearing only dog-tags and
boxers, waters it. While FATIMA (70), also Arab American,
sporting a cute pink sweat-suit, prunes the tree's limbs.

                    FATIMA
          Happy Thanksgiving, Lizzy!

                    LIZZY (O.S.)
          Hey, Muhammad 'n Fatima!

                    MUHAMMAD
          Hey, Lizzy, just waterin' the pine.
          Ya know, I planted this tree when I
          got back from 'nam, the same year--

                    LIZZY (O.S.)
          You 'n Fatima got married, I know.

                    MUHAMMAD
          I've told you about my pine before?

                    FATIMA
          Yes, habibi, you've told Lizzy
          about our pine a million times.

                    MUHAMMAD
             (exploding)
          Stop telling me what I've said and
          haven't said before today, Fatima!

                    FATIMA
             (to Lizzy)
          Please forgive Muhammad's behavior,
          we forgot to refill his medication
          before the holiday, he's taken mood
          stabilizers since before the war.

                    MUHAMMAD
          Nothin's wrong with my mood, woman!

EXT. BONNIE & STEVE'S FRONT YARD - RING-SWING TREE - SAME

Bobby and Dave-O stand by the ring-swing tree. Alvin BARKS.

                    DAVE-O
             (terrified)
          Alvin's gonna bite me, Bobby!

Bobby leans down, petting Alvin. He stops barking.

> BOBBY
> Heavy pet him then he'll be nice.

> DAVE-O
> "Heavy" pet him?

> BOBBY
> "No frettin' after heavy pettin'."
> I learned it on *Rupaul's Drag Race*.

> LIZZY (O.S.)
> Bobby?

They look to

THE DRIVEWAY OF BONNIE & STEVE'S HOUSE - SAME

Lizzy still stands beside her parked car.

> LIZZY
> Give your aunt a hug.

> BOBBY (O.S.)
> I met Dave-O, Aunt Lizzy!

Bobby excitedly runs, approaching Lizzy.

> BOBBY
> I met him, Aunt Lizzy!

Bobby stops before Lizzy, he looks up to her.

> BOBBY
> (loud whisper)
> He's nicer than your last friend.

> LIZZY
> Just give me a hug, Bobby.

Bobby hugs her.

> ROBERT (O.S.)
> They're here!

INT. BONNIE & STEVE'S HOUSE - THE KITCHEN - SAME

Robert stands over the kitchen sink, looking out the KITCHEN
WINDOW. He turns to Bonnie, Steve, Jeanette, and Jenny.

                    ROBERT
          Lizzy 'n Dave-O are here.

Bonnie, Steve, and Jeannette nod. Jenny blankly stares.

                    JENNY
          Dave-O? Who is that?

                    ROBERT
          Dave-O, you met him on the
          FaceyTime call we did. Aunt Lizzy
          was there. Remember, Aunt Lizzy?

                    JENNY
               (exploding)
          I know who Aunt Lizzy is, she's my
          aunt! I don't remember any
          FaceyTime call with a Dave-O guy!

                    ROBERT
          He's Australian, remember...?

                    JENNY
          No, because I wasn't there!

                    ROBERT
          Yes, you were.

                    JENNY
          Stop gaslighting me, Dad!

                    ROBERT
          I'm not gaslighting you.

                    JEANETTE
          Yes, you are, honey.

                    ROBERT
          I am?

                    JEANETTE
          Yeah, Jenny-doll wasn't there.

                    LIZZY (O.S.)
          We're here!

Lizzy jumps into the kitchen from around the wooden corner.
Dave-O and Bobby stand at the wooden corner. They watch.

                    LIZZY
          Mom!

Lizzy excitedly hugs Bonnie then spies Steve.

                    LIZZY
          Dad!

Lizzy excitedly hugs Steve then spies Robert.

                    LIZZY
          Rob!

Lizzy excitedly hugs Robert then spies Jeanette.

                    LIZZY
          Jeanette!

Lizzy excitedly hugs Jeanette then spies Jenny.

                    LIZZY
          Jenny!

Lizzy excitedly hugs Jenny then Lizzy turns to them all.

                    LIZZY
          I'd like you all to officially meet
          my boyfriend, Dave-O. Be nice.

Dave-O steps forward.

                    DAVE-O
          G'day, everyone, how ya going?

                    BONNIE
          What kinda terrorist are you, boy?

                    DAVE-O
          That kind that terrorizes my
          friends and family with love.

Bonnie laughs as she aggressively hugs him.

                    BONNIE
          You'll fit right in, Dave-O!

Steve excitedly puts out his hand and Dave-O shakes it.

                    STEVE
          That's a good firm handshake!
          Especially for an Austrian!

                    DAVE-O
          Not Austrian, I'm from *Australia*.
          Ya know, Straya: land of *Mad Max*,
          didgeridoos, wombats, the Outback
          and all that. I'm a descendent of
          pom criminals, don't worry though,
          I honestly love your daughter, sir.

                    STEVE
          Thank the Lord somebody does, bless
          your lil' Ozzy heart, son.

                    LIZZY
               (exploding)
          Dad, I said to be nice!

                    STEVE
          Relax, I am, Tizzy-Lizzy.

                    DAVE-O
          "Tizzy-Lizzy?"

                    STEVE
          We call her that cuz she's known
          for working herself into a tizzy
          over any 'n every little thing.

                    LIZZY
          I'm never in a tizzy, Dad!

                    ROBERT
          One day, we know she'll snap.

                    JENNY
          Go full-blown cookoo-bah-dookoo.

                    BOBBY
          And kill us all in a rage-tizzy.

A wide-eyed pause from all then they break into laughter.

                    BONNIE
          Yup, dems da breaks when your
          daughter is one o' them rage-
          terrorists, part-time emotionally
          manipulative terrorist of course,
          but full-time rage-terrorist.

                    STEVE
               (back to Dave-O)
          Y'all get along, Dave-O?

                    DAVE-O
          Like a house on fire, sir, unless,
          I'm being cheeky. Ironically,
          that's how we met on holiday in
          Africa.

I was being cheeky on our animal
safari, I sure threw a spanner in
the works that day as I refused to
shoot any animals, Lizzy joined me
in my defiant protest, I was keen
to shoot a gun though, I just don't
like killing things.

                STEVE
What do you do, Dave-O?

                DAVE-O
Travel mostly.

                STEVE
But what do you do for work?

                DAVE-O
Nothing, ya see, Gran and I
inherited heaps of money when
Grandad died. He owned a gold mine.

Jenny steps up to Dave-O and he excitedly hugs her.

                DAVE-O
We finally meet, Jenny!

Jenny, still hugging Dave-O, looks to Robert.

                JENNY
See, we haven't met before.

Dave-O, still hugging Jenny, spies Robert.

                DAVE-O
Robert, there's the bloke!

Dave-O releases Jenny then he excitedly hugs Robert.

                DAVE-O
Mate, you put away more tinnies
over FaceyTime than anyone ever!

                JEANETTE
He got so drunk that night.

                DAVE-O
And you didn't, Jeanette?

Dave-O releases Robert then Dave-O excitedly hugs Jeanette.

                DAVE-O
So good to meet you in the flesh!

Dave-O releases Jeanette then looks to everyone.

                    DAVE-O
          So good to meet all of you!

Robert looks to Jenny.

                    ROBERT
          Sorry, I thought you were there,
          the FaceyTime call with Dave-O.

                    JENNY
          I'm sick of the gaslighting, Dad!

                    ROBERT
          I said, I was sorry!

Dave-O excitedly hugs them both at the same time.

                    DAVE-O
          Petty family bickering, I love it!

Bobby steps forward from the wooden corner.

                    BOBBY
          I'm hungry, can we eat now?

INT. BONNIE & STEVE'S HOUSE - DINING ROOM - MOMENTS LATER

All sit at a huge DINING ROOM TABLE. Atop the table is the
browned stuffed turkey and a juicy spiral ham (pineapple
rings and Maraschino cherries stuck to it via toothpicks).

Also atop the table, a full gravy boat rests beside a pot of
mashed potatoes, which is near a pan of whipped sweet
potatoes (topped with toasted marshmallows), and finally,
near that is some sort of cheese-covered casserole.

                    ROBERT
          Looks good!

Robert jumps up, shovelling mashed potatoes onto his plate.
Everyone snaps into it, passing each other dishes of this,
that, and the other. Steve passes Dave-O the sweet potatoes.

                    DAVE-O
          Cheers, mate.

                    STEVE
          Cheers?

                    DAVE-O
          We say "cheers" for "thanks."

                    STEVE
          Oh, we say "cheers" for toasting.
               (to himself)
          Maybe I should toast our lil'
          announcement about the farm.

                    DAVE-O
               (whispering)
          You making a toastie-woastie about
          selling the farm, sir?

                    STEVE
               (whispering back)
          How do you know about that?

                    LIZZY
               (super excited)
          Is that my hashbrown casserole?!

                    BONNIE
          Yup, it *is* your favorite, Lizzy.

Lizzy plops some onto her plate then some onto Dave-O's.

                    DAVE-O
          Save some room for the turkey and
          the glistening gravy, babes.

                    ROBERT
          We'll have turkey after our break.

                    DAVE-O
          Sorry, Robert?

                    ROBERT
          We eat, first round ya know, then
          take a break with football--

                    DAVE-O
          Footy?

                    ROBERT
          No, 'merican football, then we come
          back 'n eat some more, round two.
          That's when we carve the turkey.

                    DAVE-O
          I've never had turkey before.

All, except Lizzy, stop and turn, staring at Dave-O in shock.

                    BONNIE
          Never?

                    LIZZY
          No, he's pretty fresh to America 'n
          turkey is an American bird, that's
          Dave-O's dream though, having a
          plate of turkey covered in
          glistening gravy all to himself.
          It's always in our holiday movies.
               (turning to Dave-O)
          Wait 'til you have it with
          cranberry sauce, babe, so good.

                    BONNIE
               (realizing)
          I forgot to put it on the table.

                    LIZZY
          Huh?

                    BONNIE
          The cranberry sauce, I forgot it.

                    STEVE
          Big surprise.

                    BONNIE
               (snapping)
          I didn't forget it totally, it's
          ready, just in the fridge!

                    ROBERT
               (exploding)
          No bickering!

                    LIZZY
          Yeah, this is Thanksgiving dinner
          'n we have a guest!

                    BONNIE
          We're not bickering, kids, we're
          fighting because we're getting a...

Bonnie can't finish so Steve gives her an encouraging nod.

                    STEVE
          Go ahead, just like we practiced.

                    BONNIE
          We're getting a...

Bonnie stares at Bobby who innocently stares back.

                    BONNIE
          I can't in front of the grands.

                    BOBBY
          What kind of cranberry sauce did
          you forget to put on the table,
          Mamaw?

                    BONNIE
          Don't worry, it's the canned kind.

                    JENNY
          I'll get it from the fridge, Mamaw.

                    DAVE-O
          Aw, "Mamaw," I'll help.

Jenny and Dave-O stand then both head off, meeting at

THE KITCHEN - REFRIGERATOR - SAME

Jenny opens the refrigerator door, Dave-O standing beside
her. Jenny grabs a plate of cut canned cranberry sauce.

                    DAVE-O
          This is a big dinner for me.

                    JENNY
          Cuz you've never had turkey before?

                    DAVE-O
          No, I'm proposing to Aunt Lizzy.

Jenny drops the plate but Dave-O catches it.

                    JENNY
          Do you have a ring?

                    DAVE-O
          Sure do.

Dave-O pulls a small velvety closed box from his pocket.

                    JENNY
          Can I hold it?

                    DAVE-O
          'Course.

He gives her the box. Jenny flips it open--a gold-diamond-
ring. She flips it closed then puts the box into her pocket.

                    JENNY
          When you ask for her hand, I'll
          present the ring to Aunt Lizzy.

Jenny grabs the plate of cranberry sauce and takes it into

THE DINING ROOM - SAME

Jenny places the plate of cranberry sauce onto the table and
sits with her family. Dave-O returns also, sitting by Lizzy.

                    STEVE
          I have an announcement.

All look to Steve who stands up as he CLINKS his glass.

                    STEVE
          Your mother 'n I are divorcing,
          we've already sold the farm too.

Robert and Lizzy look to Bonnie.

                    ROBERT
          Is that true, Mom?

                    LIZZY
          Yeah, are you really divorcing?

                    BONNIE
          I can't do this.

                    STEVE
          Yes, you can.

                    BONNIE
          No, I can't, this is too messed up,
          especially in front of the grands!

                    BOBBY
          Aw, I wanted two Christmases.

                    JENNY
          What do you mean, Bobby?

                    BOBBY
          Well, if Mamaw 'n Papaw were
          getting a divorce that'd mean we'd
          get two Christmases every year
          until one of 'em is dead. That's
          what my friend, Chason Smith, got
          until his grandpa died, so cool.

                    BONNIE
          Ya mean, if we got a divorce, it
          wouldn't bother you, Bobby?

                    BOBBY
               (super excited)
          No, it'd mean two Christmases!

                    JENNY
          It doesn't bother me either, Mamaw,
          nothing lasts, in fact, I just
          dumped my boyfriend, he gaslit.

                    STEVE
          See, the grands'll be fine.

                    BONNIE
          Then we're divorcing, dear.

                    ROBERT
          Well, I'll be damned if we're going
          to two Christmases this year, I
          don't think it's "so cool!"

                    LIZZY
          Yeah, not "so cool" at all!

Robert and Lizzy angrily stand, leaving the table and the
dining room in a huff. They EXIT out into the front yard.

EXT. BONNIE & STEVE'S HOUSE - FRONT YARD - MOMENTS LATER

Robert tosses a football up and down to himself.

                    ROBERT
          Those old kooks are crazy if they
          think I'm doing Christmas twice.

                    LIZZY (O.S.)
          Toss me the ball, bro.

Reveal that Lizzy stands nearby on the lawn. Over on the
tree, Bobby ring-swings, Dave-O stands beside him watching.

                    LIZZY
          Toss me the ball, bro!

Robert throws the football to Lizzy.

                    ROBERT
          You got a plan don't ya, sis?

                    LIZZY
          A plan?

                    ROBERT
          To get the old kooks back together.

                    LIZZY
          Like our Parent Trap Christmas?

Lizzy throws the football to Robert.

                    ROBERT
          What're you talking about?

                    LIZZY
          When we were little 'n they
          separated like for a day 'n we
          pulled our Parent Trap Christmas.
          It was Christmas time, remember...?

                    ROBERT
               (remembering)
          Oh, yeah!

                    LIZZY
          I knew we had 'em once Mom started
          calling Dad "dear" again.

                    ROBERT
          You know Mom just called Dad "dear"
          as in "we're divorcing, dear."

Robert throws the football to Lizzy.

                    LIZZY
          You think Mom's lying about 'em
          getting a divorce?

                    ROBERT
          I wouldn't be surprised, I bet Dad
          manipulated her into saying it.

                    LIZZY
          Why?

Lizzy throws the football to Robert.

                    ROBERT
          Notice how Dad just slipped in the
          part about the farm being sold
          after he announced their "divorce?"

                    LIZZY
          He did just slip it in there, so?

                    ROBERT
          He promised the farm to me.

                    LIZZY
                 (exploding)
          Me too! That promise-liar!

                    ROBERT
          I don't want it, you can have it.

                    LIZZY
          It's already been sold!

                    ROBERT
          Why did you want the farm so bad?

Robert throws the football to Lizzy.

                    LIZZY
          Cuz after I marry Dave-O--

                    ROBERT
          Dave-O proposed?

                    LIZZY
          No.

                    ROBERT
          Oh.

                    LIZZY
          Anyhow, after I marry Dave-O, we
          woulda lived here, had crops 'n
          raised livestock, everything we ate
          woulda been super-duper organic.
          That's my forever dream, it was.

                    ROBERT
          Bye-bye forever dream.

                    LIZZY
          Yup, bye-bye forever dream.

Lizzy throws the football to Robert.

                    ROBERT
          Be funny if Dad made-up the divorce
          'n suckered Mom into going along
          just to distract us from the sale.

Robert throws the football to Lizzy.

                    LIZZY
          How do you mean?

> ROBERT
> I mean Dad sold the farm then
> remembered he promised it to us--

> LIZZY
> --and instead of facing the broken
> promises he made-up the divorce so--

> ROBERT
> --we'd be too shocked to freak-out.

> LIZZY
> Whopper, classic Dad move.

> ROBERT
> Happy Thanksgiving, sis.

Jeanette and Jenny come out of the house, joining them.

> JEANETTE
> Robert, your face is flushed, do
> your breathing exercises, honey.

> LIZZY
> Breathing exercises?

> ROBERT
> For my panic attacks, sis.

Jenny runs over to the

RING-SWING TREE - SAME

Bobby still swings, Dave-O still watching. Jenny pulls out
the velvety closed ring box and hands it to Dave-O.

> JENNY
> What're you gonna do now, Dave-O?

> DAVE-O
> What do you mean, mate?

> JENNY
> You can't ask Aunt Lizzy to marry
> you now that Mamaw 'n Papaw are
> divorcing, they've ruined it.

Bobby jumps down off the ring-swing, he stares at the velvety
box in Dave-O's hand. Dave-O opens it, showing off the ring.

> BOBBY
> Is that ring for Aunt Lizzy?

                    DAVE-O
          Sure is, it's a secret though.

Dave-O closes the box then hands it back to Jenny.

                    JENNY
          What're you giving it to me for?

                    DAVE-O
          When I ask for Aunt Lizzy's hand in
          marriage, you'll present the ring.

                    JENNY
          You're still gonna ask her?

                    DAVE-O
          Yep, over the weekend, I have
          another surprise for her too.

                    JENNY
          What?

                    DAVE-O
          I bought Mamaw and Papaw's farm.
          The money hasn't gone from my
          account yet but I bought it.

                    JENNY
          It will.

                    DAVE-O
          Sorry?

                    JENNY
          The money will go from your
          account, the banks are closed 'n
          it's probably just messing with
          your account. Thanksgiving.

                    DAVE-O
          'Course, Thanksgiving.

                    BOBBY
          What do I do for your marriage
          proposal, Dave-O?

                    DAVE-O
          What do you mean, mate?

                    BOBBY
          I mean, Jenny's holding 'n
          presenting the ring. What's my job?

                    DAVE-O
          Your job is super-dupery important.

                    BOBBY
          It is? What is it?

                    DAVE-O
          If Aunt Lizzy gives me any guff
          during the proposal you're to
          remind her what a stand-up bloke I
          am, she'll listen to you cuz she
          wants to eat you up with a side of
          ketchup. You're that cute, mate.

                    BOBBY
          But what if you're a bad bloke?

                    DAVE-O
          Sorry?

                    BOBBY
          What if you're not a "stand-up"
          bloke but a bad one. You seem nice,
          but I don't know you at all.

                                        BACK TO:

THE FRONT YARD - SAME

Lizzy, Robert, and Jeanette still stand in the yard.

                    JEANETTE
          They're lying about getting a
          divorce? What're y'all gonna do?

                    ROBERT
          Nothing, honey. Lizzy, the ball.

Lizzy looks down, staring at the football in her hands.

                    LIZZY
          Let's do Christmas now.

Lizzy throws the football to Robert.

                    ROBERT
          Whataya mean "do Christmas now?"

Robert throws the football back to Lizzy.

                         LIZZY
          We'll do Christmas now, it's the
          last time we can do it on the farm.
          Plus, Mom 'n Dad hate Christmas.

                         ROBERT
          Payback, huh?

                         LIZZY
          Exactly, payback for killing my
          forever dream of owning the farm.

Lizzy throws the football to Jeanette.

                         JEANETTE
          Also if we do Christmas now, we
          won't have to do it later, I'm in.

INT. BONNIE & STEVE'S HOUSE - DINING ROOM - SAME

Steve and Bonnie sit at the DINING ROOM TABLE, the
Thanksgiving spread still rests atop it.

                         STEVE
          Do you like how I just slipped in
          the "already sold the farm" part?

                         BONNIE
          You're still very clever, dear.

                         STEVE
          I hope your use of the word "dear"
          didn't tip-off the kids.

                         BONNIE
          Did I say "dear" when I said "we're
          getting a divorce?" Sorry, dear.

                         STEVE
          Check our bank account again to see
          if the sale money has shown up yet.

Bonnie looks to her iphone in hand--their bank account page:
$2.98. She hits refresh on the page. It comes back up: $2.98.

                         BONNIE
          Nope, it still hasn't shown up yet.
          When should we "get back together"
          for "the good of the family," dear?

                    STEVE
          Well, I won't believe our sale's
          legit until the money shows up so
          we'll have to keep pretending we're
          getting a divorce until then.

                    BONNIE
          That could be all weekend.

                    STEVE
          So be it.

                    BONNIE
          But why?!

                    STEVE
          Cuz if the sale's not legit, I
          gotta try to sell the farm again.

                    BONNIE
          So?

                    STEVE
          I gotta be under the spell of
          "divorce-fueled-passion" when I do.

                    BONNIE
          So we can't "get back together?"

                    STEVE
          Not until the money shows up in our
          account or I clench another sale.

                    BONNIE
          Just tell 'em the truth, that you
          bought a condo 'n we're gonna spend
          our golden years down in Florida.

                    STEVE
          No, I can't face 'em without hiding
          behind "divorce-fueled-passion." I
          can't face another promise-lie come
          to light without a good excuse,
          especially one this big. They'll
          write us off forever 'n we'll never
          see the grands again. Never-ever.

EXT. BONNIE AND STEVE'S HOUSE - THE FRONT YARD - SAME

Lizzy, Jeanette, and Robert stand on the grassy lawn.

                    JEANETTE
          Well, let's end Thanksgiving 'n get
          started on Christmas then, y'all.

Jeanette throws the football to Robert as Bobby marches over.

                    BOBBY
               (angry)
          You said, I could play football
          after Thanksgiving dinner, Dad!

                    ROBERT
          Thanksgiving dinner's not over yet,
          son. This was just our usual "round
          one" break. Thanksgiving's not over
          until the turkey's carved all up.

INT. BONNIE & STEVE'S HOUSE - DINING ROOM - MOMENTS LATER

The entire family, including Dave-O, surround the DINING ROOM
TABLE again. Robert stands at the table, carving the turkey.

                    STEVE
               (angry)
          That's my job, son!

                    ROBERT
          It was your job, Dad! I'm the man
          of the house now at Thanksgiving
          since you 'n Mom are divorcing!
               (smiling and to Dave-O)
          Dave-O, ready for some turkey?

                    DAVE-O
               (super excited)
          Yes, heaps, please!

Robert nods then hands Dave-O a heaping plate of turkey. Dave-
O happily stares at the heaping plate of turkey in his hands.

                    LIZZY (O.S.)
          You'll want gravy, babe.

He looks to his right. Lizzy sits, holding the gravy boat.

                    LIZZY
          Mom's turkey is always dry.

                    BONNIE
          Hey.

Lizzy pours glistening gravy all over Dave-O's turkey.

                    DAVE-O
Dream fulfilled! Tick!

                    LIZZY
Hey, Mom 'n Dad, since you're
divorcing 'n the farm is already
sold, we thought we'd do Christmas
this weekend. Whataya think?

                    STEVE
          (suspicious)
Why?

                    LIZZY
This is the last time we can do
Christmas on the farm. It's sold.
Plus, if we do Christmas now, we
won't have to do it this year at
all 'n I bet you 'n Mom will be
really busy next month meeting with
lawyers 'n whatnot.

                    STEVE
Oh, right.

                    BOBBY
Aw, I wanted two Christmases, Aunt
Lizzy, I never get what I want.

                    LIZZY
But you'll get all your presents
from everyone now. Who even knows
if you'd get 'em all later, one of
these old kooks could die by then.

                    BONNIE
Hey, don't speak to him like that.

                    STEVE
Yeah.

                    LIZZY
It's the truth, either of you could
be dead by Christmas. Divorces are
very stressful, heart attack
inducing type stress. It's just the
truth. You both remember what
telling the truth is like, right?

                    JENNY
          (getting excited)
Is there gonnna be Christmas
presents 'n all, Aunt Lizzy?!

                    LIZZY
          'Course, Black Friday is tomorrow.

                    JENNY
          I want Cowgirly boots!

                    ROBERT
          What are "Cowgirly" boots?

                    JEANETTE
          They're the new thing, honey.

                    JENNY
          They come with spurs attached!

                    ROBERT
          Great, I can hear them jingle-
          jangle-jingle twenty-four-seven.

INT. LIZZY'S ROOM - NIGHT

Lizzy's childhood bedroom--tattered posters of a teenage
Timberlake line the walls and a toy chest rests in the
corner. In the bed, sheets around them, lie Lizzy and Dave-O.

                    LIZZY
               (super excited)
          It's gonna be torturous, stuffing
          Christmas into the three day
          weekend! Black Friday, sledding,
          Christmas dinner, and the bonfire!

                    DAVE-O
          What if they really are getting a
          divorce? Aren't you concerned?

                    LIZZY
          They're not getting a divorce.

                    DAVE-O
          How do you know?

                    LIZZY
               (exploding)
          Cuz I know my Dad! He just told
          this "divorce" whopper in an
          attempt to distract us from the
          truth! He sold the farm 'n he's too
          much of a pansy to own up to his
          promise-lie! Mom's helping him!

                    DAVE-O
          Perfectly messed up for each other.

                    LIZZY
          Huh?

                    DAVE-O
          Your parents are perfectly messed
          up for each other, you're entire
          family too. You think I'll fit in?

                    LIZZY
          I think so.

                    DAVE-O
          How're we gonna sled without snow?

                    LIZZY
          What?

                    DAVE-O
          You said, "sledding." How're we
          gonna sled without snow?

                    LIZZY
          A Christmas miracle.

                    DAVE-O
          A Christmas miracle?

                    LIZZY
          Everything starts tomorrow, so be
          ready, Black Friday at GallMart.

She leans over him, CLICKING off the bedside lamp. It's DARK.

EXT. GALLMART PARKING LOT - SUNNY DAY

Robert, Jeanette, Lizzy, Steve, Bonnie, and Dave-O stand by
Robert's parked SUV, staring at the MASSES entering GallMart.

                    BONNIE
          Why didn't we bring the grands?

                    LIZZY
          Cuz we're getting presents for 'em.

                    STEVE
          But we still coulda used 'em.

                    LIZZY
          Used 'em?

                    BONNIE
          They're small.

                    LIZZY
          So?

                    STEVE
          So they coulda squeezed past all
          these jerks 'n gotten anything we
          wanted like lil' shopping ninjas.

                    ROBERT
          When do we eat?

                    STEVE
          The McDonald's inside should be
          pretty clear by now, it's three.

                    DAVE-O
          There's a Macca's inside?

                    STEVE
          "Macca's?" The hell is that?

                    DAVE-O
          I've never been to GallMart before.

All, except Lizzy, look to Dave-O in shock.

                    LIZZY
               (smugly)
          We only shop at Organic Foods.

                    STEVE
          But GallMart is so cheap.

                    BONNIE
          Yeah, if this is your first time,
          Dave-O, you should just have fun.

                    STEVE
          Yeah, shop from the hip.

                    LIZZY
               (exploding)
          No shopping from the hip! He's
          getting s'mores stuff for the
          Christmas bonfire, Dad's getting
          Cowgirly boots for Jenny, Mom's
          getting a football for Bobby, Rob's
          getting prime rib for Christmas
          dinner, Jeanette's getting--

                    BONNIE
          We don't care for prime rib.

                    STEVE
          Yeah, we hate it.

                    LIZZY
          No bickering! Now, Jeanette you're
          getting stocking stuffers 'n I'm
          getting Christmas wrapping paper!
          Does anyone have any questions
          about what they're getting?!

All shake their heads. Lizzy calms.

                    LIZZY
          Okay, see you guys in there.

Lizzy chucks Dave-O on the shoulder then she goes, joining
the masses and ENTERING the GallMart. Steve looks to Dave-O.

                    STEVE
          You should still shop from the hip.

                    BONNIE
          One of us can get s'mores stuff.

                    DAVE-O
          What do you mean shop from the hip?

                    JEANETTE
          Get whatever you want, it's cheap.

                    DAVE-O
          Cheap?

                    ROBERT
          And this place has everything, Dave-
          O, you can even turn yourself into
          the greatest cinematic character of
          all time--the Verminator.

                    DAVE-O
              (switching to an Arnold
               Schwarzeneggerish accent)
          "I need your clothes, your boots,
          and your motorcycle, baby-cakes."

The family laughs. Robert lights up, looking to Dave-O.

                    ROBERT
          You know *The Verminator*?!

                    DAVE-O
              (still Schwarzeneggerish)
          Affirmative, it stars the greatest
          actor of all time--

ROBERT	DAVE-O
Arnie Von Doomenheimer!	Arnie Von Doomenheimer!

                    ROBERT
          A fan of *The Terminator* at all?

                    DAVE-O
          (dropping the
           Schwarzeneggerish accent)
          Terrible, James Cameron's a hack.

                    DAVE-O
          Agreed, he got lucky with *Aliens*.
          Here's a lil' known fact about *The
          Verminator* series a lot of people
          don't know. It's the only movie
          franchise Gallmart's ever produced.

Dave-O looks to Gallmart in awe.

                    DAVE-O
          I didn't know that.

                    STEVE
          The Verminator is Rob's favorite.

                    BONNIE
          I still remember when I took him to
          see V2 at the theater back in '92.

                    JEANETTE
          Robert has all the collectables.

                    ROBERT
          Dave-O, at Gallmart, you can make
          yourself into the V-800 while
          drinking a Dr. Plopper.

                    DAVE-O
          What's a Dr. Plopper?

                    ROBERT
          It's like a Dr. Pepper but it's a
          Savin'-some product.

                    DAVE-O
          Savin'-some?

                    ROBERT
          GallMart's generic brand.

                    JEANETTE
          It's cheap.

                    ROBERT
          Dave-O, you can get a Dr. Plopper,
          sunglasses, a black biker outfit,
          boots, a motorcycle, and a pump-
          action shotgun for five thousand
          dollars on a non-black-Friday. Who
          knows what deals you'll find today.

                    DAVE-O
          Have you actually bought the stuff
          whenever you became the V-800?

                    ROBERT
          No, I've just priced stuff, I've
          never actually bought anything.

                    DAVE-O
          How come?

                    ROBERT
          I'm not allowed.

                    DAVE-O
          Why not?

                    JEANETTE
          It's frivolous spending.
             (smiling and to Robert)
          No browsing shotguns today, honey.

                    DAVE-O
          I've never shot a gun before.

All turn, staring at Dave-O in shock.

MONTAGE OF DAVE-O SHOPPING FROM THE HIP IN GALLMART--

--At a crowded soda dispenser, Dave-O fills up a Dr. Plopper.

--In a crowded "Sporting Goods" section, a GALLMART EMPLOYEE
(his nametag says "DELBERT") cocks a pump-action twelve gauge
shotgun for a bug-eyed Dr. Plopper slurping Dave-O.

--At a crowded sunglasses rack Dave-O stands, Dr. Plopper in
one hand, shotgun in the other. He stares at the sunglasses.

--In a crowded aisle Dave-O stands, sporting sunglasses, his
Dr. Plopper in one hand and his shotgun in the other.

                    DAVE-O
             (Schwarzeneggerish accent)
          Now for za clothes, za boots, and
          za motorcycle.

                    LIZZY (O.S.)
          No shopping from the hip!

Dave-O turns. Lizzy stands beside him, her arms crossed.

                    LIZZY
          Go get the s'mores stuff, V-800!

INT. GALLMART - GIRLS' FOOTWEAR SECTION - SAME

In a shoe aisle containing EMPTY shelves Steve stands before
a PODUNK WOMAN holding TWO SHOE BOXES, size 8.

                    STEVE
          Do you really need two boxes of
          Cowgirly Boots, size eight?

                    PODUNK WOMAN
          They's *Cowsurly* Boots.

                    STEVE
          Cowsurly Boots?

                    PODUNK WOMAN
          Savin'-some brand.

                    STEVE
          They still come attached with spurs
          that jingle-jangle-jingle, right?

                    PODUNK WOMAN
          Yes 'n I needs both boxes.

                    STEVE
          You got two girls?

                    PODUNK WOMAN
          No, I needs extra for when they's
          all sold out, like now, 'n folks
          are real desperate to get 'em.

                    STEVE
               (sighing)
          How much are they?

The Podunk Woman looks at one of the boxes.

                    PODUNK WOMAN
          "Nineteen ninety-nine."

                    STEVE
          I'll give you forty dollars for
          'em, you won't get a better deal.

INT. GALLMART - ATHLETIC SECTION - SAME

Bonnie stands before a huge EMPTY basket--a sign attached
says, "Footballs." A PODUNK MAN stands, FOOTBALL in hand.

                    BONNIE
          That's the last football 'n my
          grandson wants one for Christmas.

                    PODUNK MAN
          You gots time, grandma.

                    BONNIE
          But Christmas is this weekend.

                    PODUNK MAN
          Wuh?

                    BONNIE
          I'll give you ten dollars for it.

                    PODUNK MAN
          No deal, gots another offer?

Bonnie PUNCHES him square in the face. Stunned, he stares.

                    BONNIE
          I don't negotiate with terrorists,
          especially the haggling kind.

INT. GALLMART - FOOD AISLE - SAME

Dave-O stands before a section labeled "S'mores Supplies," he
holds a shopping basket containing Graham crackers, Mega
Marshmallows, and Hershey bars. He puts his sunglasses on.

                    DAVE-O
              (Schwarzeneggerish accent)
          Now back to shopping from za hip.

MONTAGE OF DAVE-O SHOPPING FROM THE HIP INSIDE GALLMART--

--In a crowded MENS' CLOTHING aisle amongst the "Pleather"
section Dave-O stands before a BLACK BIKER OUTFIT.

--In a crowded MENS' FOOTWEAR aisle amongst the "Boots"
section Dave-O, now in the black biker outfit (tags still
attached), stands before some BLACK BIKER BOOTS on display.

--At a crowded AUTOMOTIVE counter Dave-O stands, still in his
black biker outfit and now in the black biker boots also.

EXT. GALLMART PARKING LOT - MOMENTS LATER

Robert, Jeanette, Lizzy, Steve, and Bonnie all stand near
Robert's parked SUV, holding "GallMart" sacks. From Lizzy's
sack protrudes a tube of candy-cane covered wrapping paper.

                    LIZZY
          I got the Christmas wrapping paper.

Jeannette holds up her "GallMart" sack.

                    JEANETTE
          I got the stocking stuffers.

Robert holds up his "GallMart" sack.

                    ROBERT
          I got the prime rib.

Steve holds up his "GallMart" sack.

                    STEVE
          I got Jenny's *Cowsurly* Boots,
          better be the same as *Cowgirly*. I
          had to pay triple for 'em but
          anything for my granddaughter.

Bonnie holds up her "GallMart" sack, she has a BLACK-EYE.

                    BONNIE
          I got Bobby's football.

                    STEVE
          What happened to your eye?

                    BONNIE
          You know I don't negotiate with
          terrorists, besides I'll do
          anything for my number two grand.

                    LIZZY
          Mom, don't you think it's messed up
          to call Bobby your "number two?"

                    BONNIE
          It's not a ranking system, I call
          him that cuz he was born second.

                    ROBERT
          Dave-O actually purchased it all.

                    LIZZY
     What?

Robert points to the

EXIT/ENTRANCE OF GALLMART - SAME

Dave-O wearing sunglasses, the black biker outfit, and boots
walks from the EXIT/ENTRANCE. He heads toward them, carrying
a "GallMart" sack in one hand and his shotgun in the other.

                    ROBERT (O.S.)
          He became the V-800, Cybermorph
          Systems' model 800. His mission?
          Protect a thirteen-year-old Wan
          Bonner from Cybermorph's liquid
          metal upgrade known as the V-1000.

Dave-O continues to walk into

THE GALLMART PARKING LOT - SAME

Dave-O joins Robert, Jeanette, Lizzy, Steve, and Bonnie who
all continue to stand beside Robert's parked SUV.

                    DAVE-O
          How ya going? I mean...
               (switching to a
                Schwarzeneggarish accent)
          Salutations, human vermin.

                    ROBERT
          Where's your motorcycle, V-800?

                    DAVE-O
          I had to order za Harley, it will
          arrive at my residence in
          approximately two veeks.

                    LIZZY
          You bought a Harley Davidson?

                    DAVE-O
               (dropping the
                Schwarzeneggarish accent)
          No, a Harley Savin'-some, babes.

                    ROBERT
          You actually bought it, Dave-O?

                    DAVE-O
               (Schwarzneggarish accent)
          Affirmative, Robert Walton,
          altogether za purchases cost me
          sree-sousand ninety-nine dollars.

                    ROBERT
          Wow, you're way under five-thousand
          dollars, you just became my
          personal hero. Could I borrow your
          purchases sometime so I can morph
          into an amazing specimen like you?

                    DAVE-O
          Anytime, mate! I mean...
               (switching back to a
                Schwarzneggarish accent)
          Affirmative, Robert Walton.

                    BONNIE
          That's how you shop from the hip!

                    STEVE
          Yeah, nice job, Dave-O!

                    JEANETTE
          And he can shoot the shotgun!

                    LIZZY
               (erupting)
          Did y'all tell him to shop from the
          hip?! We have a Christmas list!

                    BONNIE
          This is his first time at GallMart.

                    STEVE
          Yeah, so we wanted him to have fun.

                    LIZZY
          No fun, this is Christmas!

                    DAVE-O
               (dropping the
                Schwarzeneggerish accent)
          No worries, babes.

Dave-O holds up his "GallMart" sack.

                    DAVE-O
          I got all the s'mores stuff.

                    ROBERT
          Let's put everything into my SUV.

EXT. COUNTRY ROAD - MOMENTS LATER

Robert's full SUV barrels down a sloppily paved country road.

INT. BONNIE & STEVE'S HOUSE - LIVING ROOM - EVENING

"GallMart" sacks and the shotgun rest on the floor. Reveal
that the entire Walton family and Dave-O (still in his V-800
ensemble) stand over it all. Robert grabs the shotgun.

                    LIZZY
          What're you gonna do with that?

                    ROBERT
          We're gonna take Dave-O to shoot.

                    LIZZY
               (exploding)
          But we got Christmas stuff to do!

                    ROBERT
          Dave-O's never shot a gun before.

                    JEANETTE
          And he's got to, he's our guest.

                    STEVE
          Yup, our guest.

                    BOBBY
          I wanna shoot too, Mamaw.

                    BONNIE
          Okay, my number two.

                    JENNY
          Me too, Mamaw.

                    BONNIE
          We'll all go 'n shoot, grands.

                    LIZZY
               (aggressive whine)
          What about me?!

                    STEVE
          What about you?

                    LIZZY
          You're all gonna go shoot the
          shotgun 'n leave me to do Christmas
          stuff all by myself!

                    DAVE-O
          I'll stay with you, babes.

                    JEANETTE
          No, you have to go, Dave-O.

                    ROBERT
          I'll tell you what, sis, we'll bag
          a tree while we're gone shooting.

                    LIZZY
          Bag a tree?

Robert loads red shells into the shotgun.

                    ROBERT
          While we're gone you get the
          ornaments for the tree 'n other
          Christmas stuff down then when we
          get back we'll decorate the tree.

                    LIZZY
          Okay.

                    ROBERT
          It's a plan then.

Robert pumps the shotgun.

EXT. THE WOODS - NIGHT

Dave-O (still in his V-800 ensemble), Robert (shotgun in
hand), Jeanette, Bobby, Jenny, Bonnie, Alvin, and Steve walk.

                    ROBERT
          So, why are you getting a divorce?

                    STEVE
          Uh, sex-life, son.

                    ROBERT
          Sex-life?

                    BONNIE
          Lack of sex-life, son.

                    BOBBY
          What's that mean, Mamaw?

                    ROBERT
          You don't wanna hear that, Bobby.

                    BOBBY
          I don't?

                    ROBERT
          No, trust me.

Suddenly Alvin GROWLS, staring up at Dave-O. They all stop.

                    STEVE
          What's gotten into Alvin?

                    BOBBY
          He doesn't know Dave-O yet.

                    DAVE-O
               (Schwarzneggerish accent)
          Canines behave savagely in za
          presence of all Verminators.

Bobby leans down, petting Alvin. He stops growling.

                    BOBBY
          "No frettin' after heavy pettin'."

                    ROBERT
          That doesn't mean what you think.

                    BOBBY
          It doesn't, Dad?

                    JEANETTE
          Is that a good one, honey?

Jeanette points--all look to a small standing pine tree.

                    ROBERT
          Yes, that one's perfect, honey.
          Dave-O, you ready to shoot?

                    JENNY
          You said, I could shoot first, Dad.

                    ROBERT
          No, I didn't.

                    JENNY
               (exploding)
          Stop gaslighting me!

                    ROBERT
          Dave-O's never shot a gun before!
               (smiling and to Dave-O)
          Dave-O, you ready?

                    DAVE-O
          Heaps ready, I mean...
               (switching back to a
                Schwarzneggerish accent)
          Affirmative, Robert Walton.

Robert hands Dave-O the shotgun.

> ROBERT
> Careful it's loaded 'n ready.

Dave-O aims for the standing small pine tree.

> ROBERT
> Aim for the trunk.

Dave-O adjusts, aiming for the tree's trunk.

> JEANETTE
> Tuck the butt into your shoulder
> more, it's gonna kick.

Dave-O adjusts, tucking the butt into his shoulder more.

> DAVE-O
> (Schwarzneggerish accent)
> Hasta la vista, baby-cakes.

Dave-O squeezes the trigger--BLAM.

INT. MUHAMMAD & FATIMA'S HOUSE - BEDROOM - SAME

In bed, Muhammad wakes. By his side is Fatima, already awake.

> MUHAMMAD
> (alarmed)
> Charlie is here!

> FATIMA
> No, it's just shotgun fire
> somewhere far off, habibi.

Muhammad jumps out of bed, he goes to their BEDROOM WINDOW.

> MUHAMMAD
> But there's people in our woods!

Fatima gets out of bed, she goes to the bedroom window also.

> FATIMA
> It's probably just the Walton grand-
> kids playing flashlight tag.

BLAM--the sound of a shotgun firing echoes.

> MUHAMMAD
> With shotguns? No, it's terrorists.

                    FATIMA
          I wish this holiday would just end
          so we could refill your meds,
          habibi, your mood's getting more
          paranoid and manic by the minute.

                    MUHAMMAD
          Nothin's wrong with my mood, woman!

INT. BONNIE & STEVE'S HOUSE - ATTIC - SAME

Lizzy, dirty, moves a dusty stack of duct-taped boxes aside,
revealing another dusty stack of duct-taped boxes. She huffs.

                    LIZZY
          Once I find the Christmas stuff,
          the torture will really start, that
          promise-liar 'n his lil' helper
          will get theirs for selling the
          farm 'n killing my forever dream.

Lizzy blows strands of hair out of her dirty face then she
moves aside the stack of dusty duct-taped boxes to reveal
another stack of dusty duct-taped boxes--"X-Mas Stuff" is
written across them in RED MARKER. Lizzy Grinchily grins.

                    LIZZY
          Mom 'n Dad hate Christmas.

INT. BONNIE & STEVE'S HOUSE - LIVING ROOM - LATER

A decorated SMALL CHRISTMAS TREE stands in the corner.

                    ROBERT (O.S.)
          Tree's done!

Reveal that Robert, the rest of the Walton family, and Dave-O
stand. Lizzy stands over an open "X-Mas Stuff" box.

                    LIZZY
          Whataya mean done?

                    ROBERT
          I mean the tree can't hold anymore
          ornaments, it's done.

                    LIZZY
              (exploding)
          But we haven't used any of my Troll
          Y'all ornaments!

                         DAVE-O
                   (looking to Steve)
              Troll Doll ornaments?

                         STEVE
              Not Troll Doll ornaments, Troll
              Y'all ornaments. Troll Y'alls are
              GallMart's version of Troll Dolls.
              It's all we could afford when Lizzy
              was a kid. Savin'-some. Cheap.

                         BONNIE
              She loves 'em though.

                         LIZZY
              Your tree's too small, Rob!

                         ROBERT
              No, my tree's fine, Tizzy-Lizzy!

                         LIZZY
              I got a whole box of unused
              ornaments that say different! Now,
              go out 'n bag me another tree!

                         ROBERT
              No!

                         LIZZY
              Then when we string the lights on
              the house tomorrow, you're helping
              me with my Troll Y'all Nativity!

                         ROBERT
              No, I hate doing that Nativity with
              you, it's always gotta be just so!

                         LIZZY
              Then go bag another tree!

                         ROBERT
              No!

                         LIZZY
              Troll Y'all Nativity for you then!

INT. LIZZY'S ROOM - LATER THAT NIGHT

Lizzy's childhood bedroom--tattered teenage Timberlake
posters plaster the walls and a toy chest still rests in the
corner. In the bed, sheets around them, lie Lizzy and Dave-O.

                    DAVE-O
          You're being a brat.

                    LIZZY
          What?

                    DAVE-O
          You're little warped Christmas
          revenge plan isn't working and
          you're being a brat about it.

                    LIZZY
               (exploding)
          It is so working!

                    DAVE-O
          Drop it so we can just enjoy the
          rest of the time with your family.

                    LIZZY
          No, my Dad's gotta pay!

Lizzy leans over, CLICKING off the bedside lamp. It's DARK.

EXT. BONNIE & STEVE'S HOUSE - FRONT YARD - SUNNY DAY

A LOUD MOTOR resounds as Lizzy stands in the yard.

                    LIZZY
               (shouting over the motor)
          I gotta pay what?!

Reveal that a MAN in a "Mister Snow" shirt stands before her.
Near him is a MACHINE which is the source of the loud motor
sound. It spits snow out of a tube and into the front yard.

                    MISTER SNOW
               (shouting over the motor)
          A thousand dollars, I say!

                    LIZZY
          For just the front yard?!

                    JENNY (O.S.)
          Don't let that terrorist gaslight
          you out of money, Aunt Lizzy!

                    LIZZY
          Don't worry, Jenny, I won't!

Lizzy looks over to

BONNIE & STEVE'S HOUSE - GROUND LEVEL - SAME

Jenny, Bobby, Dave-O, and Alvin stand at the base of a ladder which leans against the home's roof.

                    JENNY
          They're all a bunch of haggling,
          gaslighting, snow-hoarding jerks!

                    LIZZY (O.S.)
          I know, Jenny!

                    JEANETTE (O.S.)
          Hold the ladder, I'm coming down!

Jenny, Bobby, and Dave-O look up to the top of the ladder leaning against the roof's edge. Jeanette appears, staple gun in hand. She climbs down the ladder which the kids and Dave-O firmly hold. Jeanette reaches the ground, joining them all.

                    JEANETTE
          Your father 'n I are done stapling
          the Christmas lights to the roof,
          but he still needs to arrange the
          Troll Y'all Nativity. Lizzy always
          wants it a very particular way so
          he needs her up there with him.

                    JENNY
          Aunt Lizzy is dealing with a snow-
          hoarding terrorist right now but I
          know how she likes the nativity.

                    JEANETTE
          Go up and help your father then.

                    JENNY
          Me?! Really?!

                    STEVE (O.S.)
          Let us know when the snow's ready!

                    DAVE-O
          Sorry?!

Dave-O looks over to

THE FRONT PORCH - SAME

Steve and Bonnie stand, holding the front door open.

                    STEVE
          (cuffing his hands as he
          shouts over the motor)
     I say, let us know when the snow's
     ready!!! We're going inside!!!

                    DAVE-O (O.S.)
          'Course, no worries, sir!!!

Steve nods then looks to Bonnie.

                    STEVE
     God, I hate Christmas.

                    BONNIE
     Ditto, dear.

They ENTER the home.

INT. MUHAMMAD & FATIMA'S HOUSE - LIVING ROOM - SAME

The motor sounds as Fatima and Muhammad stand at the WINDOW.

                    MUHAMMAD
     Well played, terrorists, but you
     didn't count on me, didja?

                    FATIMA
     Terrorists? It's just the Waltons.

                    MUHAMMAD
     Terrorists are holding the Waltons
     hostage and making them do this.

                    FATIMA
     What?

                    MUHAMMAD
     That was the shotgun fire we heard
     last night, Steve put up a fight
     but he was overpowered, dead now.

                    FATIMA
     You think Steve's dead?

                    MUHAMMAD
     You don't see him do ya?

Fatima stares out the window.

                    FATIMA
     I don't see him cuz he's inside.

                    MUHAMMAD
          Inside a shallow grave, the
          terrorists blew him away with a
          shotgun last night then took the
          rest of the Walton family hostage
          and now they're making them put up
          Christmas lights and forcing snow
          to make Christmas come sooner.

                    FATIMA
          What? Why?

                    MUHAMMAD
          To confuse the American public.

                    FATIMA
          You're not making any sense.

                    MUHAMMAD
          See, it's already working, you're
          already confused and the American
          public is next with no holiday
          markers to gage time. It's a
          classic torture tactic: remove time
          from the torturee and watch him or
          her go insane. Like I say, well
          played terrorists, but don't worry
          cuz they didn't count on me
          figuring out their plan and
          stopping them before it's too late.

                    FATIMA
          God, we need to refill those meds.

                                        BACK TO:

EXT. BONNIE & STEVE'S HOUSE - FRONT YARD - SAME

Lizzy and Mister Snow continue to haggle, both standing
before the loud motor-running-snow-spitting machine.

                    LIZZY
               (shouting over the motor)
          Just come down a little!

                    MISTER SNOW
               (shouting over the motor)
          I can't, a thousand is my minimum!

                                        BACK TO:

BONNIE & STEVE'S HOUSE - GROUND LEVEL - SAME

Jeanette, Bobby, Dave-O, and Alvin stand at the base of the leaning ladder. Jeanette, Bobby, and Dave-O hold firm to it.

                    JENNY (O.S.)
          Y'all can let go now!

They look up. Jenny sits on the roof beside the ladder-top.

                    JENNY
          I'm up so y'all can let go!

They release the ladder. Dave-O looks to Bobby.

                    DAVE-O
          Well, that proves that I'm a stand-
          up bloke and not a bad one, I
          helped Jenny get atop the roof.

                    BOBBY
          That doesn't prove anything.

                    DAVE-O
          But I held the ladder, helped your
          sister safely get atop the roof.

                    BOBBY
          That's just regular ol' stand-up
          bloke stuff, I need more.

Alvin growls. Dave-O pets him. He stops growling.

                    DAVE-O
          Alvin likes me now. Does that prove
          to you that I'm a stand-up bloke?

                    BOBBY
          No, you just heavy petted him like
          I told you to.

                    DAVE-O
          No, I *regular* petted him, Bobby.

                    BOBBY
          No, you *heavy* petted him, Dave-O.

                    DAVE-O
          Don't know what that means, 'ey?

                    BOBBY
          It doesn't mean what I think?

                    DAVE-O
          No, mate.

                    BOBBY
          What does it mean then, Dave-O?

Dave-O looks to Jeanette who nods.

EXT. BONNIE & STEVE'S HOUSE - ROOF - SAME

The roof is covered in stapled-down strings of Christmas
lights. Robert sits before an open "X-MAS STUFF" box. Beside
that stands the Troll Y'all Manger Scene: overly fuzzy-headed
animals and overly fuzzy-headed prayer-handed shepherds stare
down at a bassinet containing an overly fuzzy headed baby.

Jenny stands, staring down at Robert and the manger scene.

                    JENNY
          Hey, Dad.

Robert looks up.

                    ROBERT
          Where's Lizzy?

                    JENNY
          Haggling with some snow-hoarding
          terrorist.

                    ROBERT
          Oh.

                    JENNY
          I know how she likes the Nativity
          manger to be arranged though.

                    ROBERT
          You're gonna help me with it?

She nods. He smiles.

                    JENNY
          First off, the sheep go on the
          other side of the shepherds.

                    ROBERT
          Okay.

He moves a herd of overly fuzzy-headed sheep from one side of
the prayer-handed overly fuzzy-headed shepherds to the other.

                    JENNY
          Dad, how come you gaslight me?

                    ROBERT
          I told ya, it's not on purpose, I
          just don't remember every little
          thing you do. So, when you think
          I'm gaslighting you about
          something, it's because I really
          don't remember that something.

                    JENNY
          How do I know you're not
          gaslighting me about not always
          gaslighting me right now?

                    ROBERT
          Huh?

                    JENNY
          Move the donkey closer to the
          shepherds.

He moves an overly fuzzy-headed donkey closer to the overly
fuzzy-headed prayer-handed shepherds.

                    ROBERT
          I guess you can't.

                    JENNY
          What?

                    ROBERT
          I guess you can't know that I'm not
          gaslighting you right now about not
          always gaslighting you. You just
          gotta have faith that I love you 'n
          will always do right by you.

                    JENNY
          Lame answer, gaslighter.
               (pointing)
          Move troll baby Jesus so that the
          shepherds 'n their anipals can
          lovingly look down upon the savior.

He moves the bassinet to the center so that the overly fuzzy-
headed prayer-handed shepherds and their overly fuzzy-headed
animals are looking down upon the overly fuzzy-headed baby.

                    ROBERT
          I may not remember every little
          thing you do but it's not because I
          don't care.

I just delete the unimportant stuff
so I can have room for the more
important stuff.

                    JENNY
Huh?

                    ROBERT
I'm old, I got a lot of memories. I
only have so much room up there so
I don't keep the unimportant stuff.
I just keep the important memories.

                    JENNY
What's an important memory you keep
about me?

                    ROBERT
I got lots but I'll tell you my
favorite, the first time I saw you.

                    JENNY
The day I was born?

                    ROBERT
I thought it was weird to be so
cold 'n even snowing on that Spring
day, anyhow when you came out of
your mother 'n I saw you for the
first time, I knew then.

                    JENNY
Knew what?

                    ROBERT
The reason I existed, the reason I
was born was so you could be born.

                    JENNY
I don't want Cowgirly Boots
anymore.

                    ROBERT
Cowsurly.

                    JENNY
Huh?

                    ROBERT
Savin'-some.

                    JENNY
Right, y'all went to GallMart.

                    ROBERT
          Don't worry, they still come
          attached with spurs that jingle-
          jangle-jingle twenty-four-seven.

                                        BACK TO:

EXT. BONNIE & STEVE'S HOUSE - FRONT YARD - SAME

Lizzy and Mister Snow continue to haggle, both still standing
before the loud motor-running-snow-spitting machine.

                    LIZZY
               (shouting over the motor)
          Just come down a little!

                    MISTER SNOW
               (shouting over the motor)
          No, if I come down for you, I gotta
          come down for everybody, lady! I
          got a family to feed too ya know?!

                                        BACK TO:

BONNIE & STEVE'S HOUSE - GROUND LEVEL - SAME

Jeanette, Bobby, and Dave-O stand at the base of the ladder.

                    BOBBY
               (exploding)
          That's what heavy pettin' means?!

                    DAVE-O
          Pretty much.

                    BOBBY
          I feel like such a dummy.

                    DAVE-O
          No worries, mate, you didn't know.

                    BOBBY
          Thanks for telling me, I've been
          saying it a lot to Chason Smith.

                    DAVE-O
          Huh?

                    BOBBY
          I told Chason Smith to heavy pet
          his dog. Do you think he did?

                    DAVE-O
          Naw, he probably just regular
          petted him, that's what I did.

                    BOBBY
          I hope you're right.

                    DAVE-O
          Who's Chason Smith and why do you
          care so much about his going's on?

                    BOBBY
          Chason comes over all the time 'n
          we play Rupaul's Drag Race.

                    DAVE-O
          Your friend, 'ey?

                    BOBBY
          My best friend but I haven't been
          such a good friend to him lately.

                    DAVE-O
          Whataya mean?

                    BOBBY
          Well, when he comes over we only
          play Rupaul's Drag Race.

                    DAVE-O
          Why does that make you a bad
          friend?

                    BOBBY
          Cuz Chason likes football but we
          never play cuz I'm no good at it.
          We just play Rupaul's Drag Race.
          That's why I wanna get a football
          'n practice. So I can get good then
          when Chason comes over we can play
          football *and* Rupaul.

                    DAVE-O
          But that makes you a good friend.

                    BOBBY
          Huh?

                    DAVE-O
          Just the fact that you care and
          have thought about Chason Smith's
          feelings makes you a good friend.

                    BOBBY
          It does?

                    DAVE-O
          Yep, you're even on track to remedy
          any potential issues as we speak.

                    BOBBY
          I guess I am.

                    DAVE-O
          You're a stand-up bloke, Bobby.

EXT. BONNIE & STEVE'S HOUSE - ROOF - SAME

Jenny continues to stand, staring down at Robert who still
sits before the overly-fuzzy headed Christmas Nativity scene.

                    JENNY
          I don't want the Cowgirly Boots
          anymore because I believe you, Dad.

                    ROBERT
          Huh?

                    JENNY
          I just wanted 'em to torture you
          for always gaslighting me but I
          believe you. You're not
          gaslighting me on purpose.

                    ROBERT
          Torture me?

                    JENNY
          They have spurs that jingle-jangle-
          jingle 'n I woulda wore them twenty-
          four-seven.

                    ROBERT
          That woulda tortured me alright.

                    JENNY
          I know but don't worry, I don't
          want the boots anymore, I don't
          even like cowgirl boots, yuck.

                    ROBERT
          Papaw already bought 'em.

                    JENNY
          He did?

                    ROBERT
          Haggled some terrorist outta 'em.

                    JENNY
          Oh.

                    ROBERT
          Just look surprised when you open
          'em 'n don't worry, you only have
          to wear 'em when we visit Papaw.

                    JENNY
          I love you, Dad.

                    ROBERT
          I love you too, Jenny-doll.

He stands. She rushes over and hugs him.

EXT. BONNIE & STEVE'S HOUSE - FRONT YARD - SAME

Lizzy and Mister Snow continue to haggle, both still standing
before the loud motor-running-snow-spitting machine.

                    LIZZY
               (shouting over the motor)
          Just come down a little!

                    MISTER SNOW
               (shouting over the motor)
          Okay, nine-hundred-ninety-nine
          ninety-nine! How's that, lady?!

                    LIZZY
          That's more like it!

                    MISTER SNOW
          Huh?!

He turns off the machine, cutting the motor and snow.

                    LIZZY
          I say, that's more like it!
               (realizing she no longer
                needs to shout)
          It's a win-win deal for us.

                    MISTER SNOW
          A win-win deal for us?

                    LIZZY
          You win enough money to feed your
          family 'n I win our haggling match.

                    MISTER SNOW
          So for nine-hundred-ninety-nine
          ninety-nine we got a deal?

                    LIZZY
          Yes.

He puts out his hand and Lizzy promptly shakes it.

                    LIZZY
               (smugly)
          I just paid under a thousand
          dollars for a Christmas miracle.

Lizzy smiles, looking out across the snow-covered front yard.
Then she hands Mister Snow a credit card. He promptly swipes
it on his credit-card-swiping-machine attached to his iphone.
Lizzy bends down, packing a snowball. Then stands, looking to

THE GROUND LEVEL OF BONNIE & STEVE'S HOUSE - SAME

Jeanette, Bobby, and Dave-O still stand. Dave-O smiles down
on Bobby. Suddenly Dave-O is hit in the head by a SNOWBALL.
Dave-O leans down, packing a snowball. He stands, looking to

THE FRONT YARD - SAME

Lizzy stands. She's hit in the face by a snowball. She drops.

                    DAVE-O (O.S.)
          Sorry, babes!

Dave-O rushes to her side.

                    DAVE-O
          Did I throw it too hard?

                    LIZZY
          No, that was perfect, babe!

She throws snow in his face then begins making a snow angel.

                    LIZZY
          I told ya a Christmas miracle would
          happen 'n provide us with snow!

                    MISTER SNOW (O.S.)
          Sure, a "Christmas miracle."

They look to Mister Snow as he loads up his machine. Then
Dave-O joins Lizzy, both making snow angels now. Lizzy stops.

                    LIZZY
          We should all make a snowman.

EXT. BONNIE & STEVE'S HOUSE - FRONT YARD - LATER

A SNOWMAN stands. He has a black top-hat, coal eyes, a carrot
nose, a smiley coal mouth, and coal buttons down his front.

                    BOBBY (O.S.)
          Something's missing.

Reveal that the entire Walton family and Dave-O stand before
the snowman. Dave-O looks to Bobby who wears a wool scarf.

                    DAVE-O
          What's missing, Bobby?

                    LIZZY
               (realizing)
          Twig arms! I'll go make 'em!

Lizzy rushes off. Dave-O looks to Bobby.

                    DAVE-O
          Is that it, Bobby? Twig arms?

                    BOBBY
               (realizing)
          Oh, I know what it is!

Bobby removes his scarf then drapes it around the snowman.

                    DAVE-O
          Perfect, just like the movies!

Bobby grins as the family gives him congratulatory head-rubs.

                    JENNY
          Can we go sledding now?

EXT. BONNIE & STEVE'S HOUSE - FRONT YARD - SAME

Lizzy, Dave-O, Bobby, Jenny, Jeanette, and Robert now all sit
on a LONG BOBSLED. It rests on top of a snowy hill, facing
the street. Alvin stands beside the sled, his tail wagging.

                    LIZZY
          Y'all ready?

                    DAVE-O/BOBBY/JENNY/JEANETTE/ROBERT
          Yeah!

Lizzy leans forward and the entire sled moves forward. It heads for the road. All scream with glee. A DIRTY PICK-UP TRUCK barrels down the road. The sled is going to meet it. Dave-O sees this. Alvin, running alongside them, BARKS. Dave-O leans over, toppling their speeding sled. Alvin stops running. He licks Dave-O's face while all lie in the snow.

                    BOBBY
          That was fabtastic sledding.

Lizzy angrily stands.

                    LIZZY
          Who's the jerk that toppled us?!

                    DAVE-O
          I did cuz of the truck, babes.

                    LIZZY
          What truck?!

Behind her on the road, the dirty pick-up truck blows past.

                    BONNIE (O.S.)
          Cookie 'n hot chocolate time!

They all look to

THE FRONT PORCH - SAME

Bonnie and Steve, holding the front door open, stand.

                    BONNIE
               (cuffing her mouth)
          Come inside for Christmas cookies
          'n hot chocolate, kids!!!

INT. BONNIE & STEVE'S HOUSE - KITCHEN - EVENING

Atop the counter, Bonnie cuts Santa shapes out of sugar-cookie dough. Then she rushes over to the stove-top and stirs a big pot of hot chocolate. At the kitchen table Dave-O, Steve, and Bobby sit, cookies and hot chocolate before them.

                    BOBBY
          We drink hot chocolate after
          sledding to warm up again.

Bobby, Dave-O, and Steve sip their hot chocolates.

                    DAVE-O
          I'm warmer already.

                    BOBBY
          We have cookies too.

                    DAVE-O
          What're the cookies for, Bobby?

                    BOBBY
          Tradition silly, plus they're good.

Bobby, Dave-O, and Steve take a bite of their Santa-cookies.

                    DAVE-O
          Mmm, you're right, they are good.

                    BOBBY
          Told ya.

                    DAVE-O
          You're a lucky-ducky, Bobby.

                    BOBBY
          How come?

                    DAVE-O
          I didn't have anything like this
          growing up at Christmas time.

                    BOBBY
          You didn't?

                    DAVE-O
          No.

                    BOBBY
          What did you have, Dave-O?

                    DAVE-O
          Well, first off, it's not winter
          time in Australia at Christmas.

                    BOBBY
          It's not?

                    DAVE-O
          No, it's summer time.

                    BOBBY
          That's cookoo-bah-dookoo.

                    DAVE-O
          Sure, I'd have Christmas barbies
          with my mates and whatnot but
          Granddad was always away dealing
          with his goldmine that part of the
          year and Gran would go with him.

                    BOBBY
               (horrified)
          You mean they left you alone?!

                    DAVE-O
          'Fraid so, mate.

                    STEVE
          Well, you got us now, Dave-O, we're
          all here 'n not going anywhere.

                    DAVE-O
          Thank you, sir.

                    STEVE
          Just call me Steve.

                    LIZZY (O.S.)
          No!

Reveal that Lizzy, Jeanette, Robert, and Jenny stand in the
kitchen. Lizzy stares down at the kitchen table and Steve.

                    LIZZY
          You don't get to have a precious
          memory with your grand-kid! You're
          divorcing 'n you sold the farm!

                    STEVE
          But we're just doing Christmas
          stuff like you wanted, Lizzy.

                    BOBBY
               (exploding)
          Don't get in a tizzy, Aunt Lizzy!

                    LIZZY
          What?

                    BOBBY
          Just calm down!

                    LIZZY
          You calm down! I just spent forty-
          five minutes on twig arms that you
          didn't even end up wanting, Bobby!

                    BOBBY
          Twig arms was your idea!

                    LIZZY
          Huh?

                    BOBBY
          I already solved what was missing
          from the snowman with my scarf!

                    JENNY
          Yeah, Aunt Lizzy, don't try to
          gaslight Bobby into thinking that
          he did something wrong! He already
          fixed the snowman with his scarf
          right, Dad?! I mean, Aunt Lizzy
          shouldn't gaslight Bobby, right?!

She looks to Robert who stands, sipping his hot chocolate.

                    ROBERT
          Let's go out 'n light up the house.

EXT. BONNIE & STEVE'S HOUSE - NIGHT

The entire Walton family, Dave-O included, stand, arms
lovingly around one another staring up at the house. The
Christmas lights and Troll Y'all Nativity scene are lit up.

                    ROBERT
          Looks great, huh?!

Everyone nods in agreement except Lizzy who scowls.

                    LIZZY
          No, my manger isn't right.

INT. LIZZY'S ROOM - NIGHT

Lizzy's childhood bedroom--tattered teenage Timberlake
posters plaster the walls and a toy chest still rests in the
corner. In bed, sheets around them, lie Lizzy and Dave-O.

                    DAVE-O
          You're missing it.

                    LIZZY
          What?

                    DAVE-O
          Good times with your family.

                    LIZZY
               (exploding)
          Good times?! No, my Dad's gotta pay
          for selling the farm!

                    DAVE-O
          Don't worry about the farm.

                    LIZZY
          What?

                    DAVE-O
          Don't worry about it, it's taken
          care of so just enjoy your family
          time, it won't last forever. You're
          my family now, ya know, Lizzy?

                    LIZZY
          What do you mean?

                    DAVE-O
          I'd give back all the money I
          inherited for just one more minute.

                    LIZZY
          Huh?

                    DAVE-O
          When Granddad took me in after my
          parents died, he helped me with the
          nightmare of their deaths. Granddad
          was good to me, just like you're
          good to me. When you and I met on
          holiday you helped me with the
          nightmare of Granddad's death.

                    LIZZY
          I woke you up from that nightmare?

                    DAVE-O
          You never wake up from the
          nightmare of someone's death. You
          simply embrace it and move forward.
          You helped me do that, Lizzy.
          You're my family now and your
          family is my family now too so stop
          being a brat and start enjoying
          your time with them.

                    LIZZY
               (exploding)
          I don't negotiate with emotionally
          manipulative terrorists like you!

                    DAVE-O
          Sorry?

                    LIZZY
          Get out of my room right now!

INT. BONNIE & STEVE'S HOUSE - LIVING ROOM - MOMENTS LATER

Dave-O, still in his pajamas, sits on the couch. He is on a
FaceyTime call with GRAN (80). Her kangaroo earrings slightly
swing as she puckers her overly plump glistening lips.

                    DAVE-O
               (horrified)
          Gaw, trout-mouth.

                    GRAN
          "Trout-mouth?" Is that good?

                    DAVE-O
               (scrambling)
          Oh, yeah, it's good Gran, I mean,
          what's more natural than a trout? I
          mean, to be called "trout-mouth" is
          defo a good thing for sure, Gran.

                    GRAN
          Thanks, sweets, they do look pretty
          natch, I got 'em done yesterday.
          Graddad would never lemme get 'em,
          he thought they'd look too fake.

                    DAVE-O
          Boy, was he ever wrong.

                    GRAN
          Are you on the couch, Dave-O?

                    DAVE-O
          Yeah, Lizzy and I had a fight.

                    GRAN
          Oh.

                    DAVE-O
          I'll be at the airport tomorrow.

EXT. BONNIE & STEVE'S HOUSE - SAME

It snows hard.

EXT. BONNIE & STEVE'S HOUSE - DRIVEWAY - MORNING

It still snows as Robert puts CHAINS onto the tires of
Lizzy's car. Dave-O stands looking down and watching.

                    ROBERT
          Done!

Robert jumps up. Dave-O puts out his hand.

                    DAVE-O
          Thanks and Merry Christmas, Robert!

Robert takes his hand, shaking it.

                    ROBERT
              (Schwarzeneggerish accent)
          Merry Christmas, baby-cakes.

Dave-O jumps into the freshly chained car then drives off.

                    LIZZY (O.S.)
          You helped Dave-O leave me?!

Reveal that Lizzy, in her pajamas, stands on the front porch.

                    ROBERT
          What?

                    LIZZY
          You just helped Dave-O leave me!

                    ROBERT
          He didn't just leave you. Did he?

Lizzy marches over to Robert and punches him in the shoulder.

                    ROBERT
          Ow, why do you think he left you?

                    LIZZY
          We had a fight last night.

                    ROBERT
          Call him.

Lizzy whips out her phone, hits a number and puts the phone
to her ear. A moment then:

                    LIZZY
          It just goes to his voice mail.

                    ROBERT
          I'd say we take my SUV 'n go after
          him but no more chains.

                    LIZZY
          No more chains?

                    ROBERT
          I put the only set on your car for
          Dave-O 'n we need those chains in
          this snow storm. It's a doozy.

She explosively balls as she lowers her phone.

INT. BONNIE & STEVE'S KITCHEN - SAME

Steve and Bonnie sit at the kitchen table. Bonnie stares at
the screen of her iphone in hand.

                    BONNIE
          I guess we can "get back together"
          for the "good of the family" now.

                    STEVE
          Not until our sale money shows up
          in our bank account, dear.

                    BONNIE
          It just did, dear.

She shows off her iphone--their bank account page: $500,000.

                    STEVE
          Our "divorce" is off then?!

                    BONNIE
          Yup, golden time!

Lizzy rushes into the kitchen, wiping away tears.

                    LIZZY
          I hope you're both happy!

                    STEVE
          We are.

                    BONNIE
          Yeah, our divorce is off.

                    LIZZY
          It was never on! I know it was just
          one of your whoppers to distract us
          from the truth of selling the farm!

                    STEVE
          How did you figure it out?

                    LIZZY
          Mom said "dear" as in "we're
          divorcing, dear!"

Steve looks to Bonnie.

                    STEVE
          I told ya it was gonna 'em tip-off.

                    BONNIE
          Sorry, dear.

                    LIZZY
          Dave-O left me because of this!

                    BONNIE
          He did?

                    STEVE
          What happened?

                    LIZZY
          We had a fight about family!

                    STEVE
          Sorry, I didn't mean to ruin you 'n
          Dave-O's relationship. I just
          thought if I solely came clean
          about the farm you kids would write
          me off forever. I promised it to
          both of you 'n me selling it, well,
          I thought it'd be the promise-lie
          to end all promise-lies, the one to
          sever our ties forever. I thought
          I'd never see the grands again. So,
          I made up the divorce. Got your
          mother to go along cuz I thought
          you kids might be more apt to
          forgive me if you thought I sold
          the farm while under the spell of
          "divorce-fueled-passion."

                    ROBERT (O.S.)
          I hope you're happy, Dad!

All look to Robert who now stands in the kitchen as well.

                    ROBERT
          Now I'll never be the V-800! Dave-O
          was gonna let me borrow all his
          stuff! Hasta la vista, baby-cakes!

Robert bursts out crying. Lizzy looks to Bonnie and Steve.

                    LIZZY
          Christmas is on with a vengeance
          now! Let's go decorate the tree!

She marches out.

                    ROBERT
               (blubbering)
          We already did that, Lizzy!

                    LIZZY (O.S.)
          A new tree! A bigger one, bro!

Robert stops crying. Bonnie and Steve grow confused looks.

                    STEVE
          A new tree? A bigger one?

EXT. MUHAMMAD & FATIMA'S FRONT YARD - MOMENTS LATER

Lizzy uses a BUZZING CHAIN-SAW to cut Muhammad's pine tree.

INT. MUHAMMAD & FATIMA'S HOUSE - LIVING ROOM - SAME

Muhammad & Fatima stand before their living room window.

                    MUHAMMAD
          My pine!

                    FATIMA
          Tizzy-Lizzy's spiraling again.

                    MUHAMMAD
          Terrorists are making her do this,
          remember?! I should call the FBI!

INT. BONNIE & STEVE'S HOUSE - KITCHEN - SAME

The PHONE attached to the wall RINGS. Steve picks it up,
putting the receiver to his ear. Bonnie stands beside him.

                    STEVE
               (into phone)
          Walton residence.

INT. SMALL AIRPORT - SAME

Dave-O stands at a public phone, dirty receiver to his ear.

                    DAVE-O
               (into phone)
          Steve?

INTERCUT PHONE CONVERSATION

                    STEVE
          Dave-O?

                    BONNIE
          Ask him why he left Lizzy.

                    STEVE
          Why did you leave Lizzy?

                    DAVE-O
          I didn't leave Lizzy, I just came
          to the airport to get my Gran.

Steve covers the phone, looking to Bonnie.

                    STEVE
          He just went to the airport to get
          his grandmother.

                    BONNIE
          Why is he getting his grandmother
          from the airport?

                    STEVE
               (back into phone)
          Why are you getting your
          grandmother from the airport?

                    DAVE-O
          I've decided I want her present
          when I ask Lizzy to marry me.

Steve covers the phone, looking to Bonnie.

                    STEVE
          He's gonna propose to Lizzy.

                    BONNIE
               (super excited)
          He's gonna propose to Lizzy?!

                    STEVE
               (back into phone)
          You're gonna propose to Lizzy?!

                    DAVE-O
          If that's okay with you, sir.

Steve covers the phone, looking to Bonnie.

                    STEVE
          If that's okay with us.

                    BONNIE
          Of course it's okay!

                    STEVE
               (back into phone)
          Of course it's okay!

                    DAVE-O
          Beauty! We'll be back tonight!
          I was hoping to be back before
          Lizzy got up but Gran's flight was
          delayed because of the storm. Just
          tell Lizzy I'm out driving around
          to clear my head from our fight.

                    STEVE
          Why don't you just call her?

                    DAVE-O
          I was in such a rush this morning I
          forgot my phone.

                    STEVE
          How did you call me?

                    DAVE-O
          I called you on what is probably
          the last payphone on Earth.

                    RECORDED OPERATOR (O.S.)
          Please deposit fifty cents to
          continue this call.

                    DAVE-O
          Steve, I'm out of quarters. So--

                    RECORDED OPERATOR (O.S.)
          Goodbye.

A DIAL TONE. Steve hangs up the phone, looking to Bonnie.

                    STEVE
          He's out of quarters.

                    BONNIE
          What?

                    STEVE
          Nothing, should we tip off Lizzy in
          regards to the upcoming proposal?

                    BONNIE
          No, a proposal is a big surprise.

                    STEVE
          Then we'll keep it a secret.

Lizzy ENTERS the kitchen from around the wooden corner.

                    LIZZY
               (calm but wild-eyed)
          Time to decorate my new tree.

                    STEVE
          Are you okay, honey?

                    BONNIE
          Yeah, Lizzy, you seem like you're
          in a crazier tizzy than usual.

                    LIZZY
               (erupting)
          I'm not in a tizzy!

INT. BONNIE & STEVE'S HOUSE - LIVING ROOM - LATER

A new huge Christmas tree stands in the corner. Lizzy adds
one last "Troll Y'all" ornament to the tree.

                    LIZZY
          There, that's all of them, right?

Lizzy turns. An open box of "X-Mas Stuff" rests on the floor.
Standing over the open box is the entire Walton family.

                    ROBERT
          That's all of them. Not just the
          Troll Y'alls but all of them.

                    LIZZY
          Perfect.
               (realizing)
          Oh, I gotta check on the prime rib.

Lizzy rushes off.

                    JEANETTE
          Prime rib?

                    JENNY
          She put it in the oven earlier.

                    BOBBY
          Christmas dinner.

                    STEVE
          I hate prime rib.

                    BOBBY
          Dad, is Aunt Lizzy okay?

                    JENNY
          Yeah, is she okay?

                    ROBERT
          No, kids.

                    LIZZY (O.S.)
          Everybody get ready for dinner!

INT. BONNIE & STEVE'S HOUSE - DINING ROOM - LATER

Steve, Bonnie, Jenny, Bobby, Robert, and Jeanette sit around
the Dining Room Table. All wear their Sunday best while
staring down at the same spread as Thanksgiving dinner.

                    JENNY
          Didn't we just do this?

                    BOBBY
          Yeah, calling it "Christmas dinner"
          and adding prime rib to it doesn't
          make it different enough, I'm still
          stuffed from Thanksgiving.

                    JEANETTE
          Both of you just play along, Dave-O
          left Aunt Lizzy so she's in her
          biggest tizzy yet.

                    ROBERT
          Yeah, this is it, the day we've all
          dreaded, your Aunt Lizzy's finally
          gone full-blown cookoo-bah-dookoo.

                    BOBBY
          My God.

                    JEANETTE
          Honey, I thought y'all were always
          just joking about that.

                    ROBERT
          Well, you thought wrong, honey.

                    JENNY
          Dad, I'm scared.

                    ROBERT
          Me too but if we keep our heads,
          we'll all get through this.

                    JENNY
          How?

                    ROBERT
          Agree with everything Aunt Lizzy
          says 'n no sudden movements.

                    JENNY
          Agree with everything she says?

                    BOBBY
          'N no sudden movements?

                    ROBERT
          Yes, anything could set her off.

                    JEANETTE
          Can't we just tell her Dave-O's
          gonna propose 'n end all this?

                    STEVE
          No, we gotta keep it a secret.

                    BONNIE
          Yeah, so that it's a surprise.

                    STEVE
          I already sold the farm, I don't
          wanna mess up her proposal too.

Lizzy ENTERS from the kitchen, steaming prime rib in hand.

                    LIZZY
          Prime rib's done!

She sets it onto the table. Everyone stiffens.

                    LIZZY
          What's wrong with everybody?

                    BOBBY
          No sudden movements.

                    LIZZY
          No sudden movements?

                    JENNY
          Anything could set you off.

                    LIZZY
          Set me off? Whataya mean?

                    ROBERT
          Nothing, Lizzy, sure smells good.

Lizzy picks up a huge knife and begins cutting the prime rib.

                    LIZZY
          Sure does.

                    JEANETTE
          I agree, it smells good.

                    JENNY
          I also agree.

                    BOBBY
          Me too.

                    LIZZY
          Why are you all acting so strange?

                    BOBBY
          We're not, we're just agreeing with
          you so you don't snap 'n kill us
          all in a rage-tizzy.
               (looking to Steve)
          Smells good, right Papaw?

                    STEVE
          Yup, it sure does, Bobby.
               (looking to Bonnie)
          Smells good, right dear?

                    BONNIE
          Yup, it smells good.

                    LIZZY
          No!

Lizzy aggressively plunges the knife into the prime rib.

                    LIZZY
          You both hate prime rib!

                    BONNIE
          Yes, Lizzy, you're right, I agree
          with you, we both hate prime rib.
               (looking to Steve)
          We hate it, right dear?

                    STEVE
          Yup, we sure do.

                    LIZZY
               (calming)
          Yes, you both hate prime rib.

INT. BONNIE & STEVE'S HOUSE - LIVING ROOM - LATER

All sit around the Christmas tree. Lizzy, a SANTA HAT atop
her head, hands out STUFFED CHRISTMAS STOCKINGS to family
members. Each stocking is bedazzled with their names. After
handing all out, she still has one left: "DAVE-O." All,
except Lizzy, begin pulling gifts from their stockings.

                    ROBERT (O.S.)
          "Xanadone?" What's this?

Reveal that Robert holds a medication container, having just
pulled it from his Christmas stocking. He looks to Jeanette.

                    JEANETTE
          It's to prevent your panic attacks,
          honey. New over-the-counter pills
          from Gallmart. Savin'-some.

                    ROBERT
          Thanks, honey.

                    JEANETTE
          You're welcome, honey.

Lizzy balls, staring at the "DAVE-O" stocking in hand.

                    BOBBY
          Is Aunt Lizzy gonna snap now?

                    ROBERT
          No, son, she's crumbling.

They continue to watch as Lizzy balls, dropping to her knees.

                    BONNIE
          Open your gift, number two grand.

                    BOBBY
          Huh? Okay.

Bobby looks to a wrapped football-shaped gift on his lap.

                    BOBBY
          Wonder what it is.

                    BONNIE
               (super excited)
          Open it and find out!

Bobby excitedly tears the wrapping off to reveal a FOOTBALL.

                    BOBBY
          A football!

                    BONNIE
          I had to beat the breaks offa some
          haggling terrorist for 'em cuz I
          don't negotiate with terrorists!

                    BOBBY
          Merry Christmas, Chason Smith!

                    BONNIE
          Huh?

                    BOBBY
          I'm gonna practice until I get good
          then me 'n my best friend, Chason
          Smith, are gonna play football!

                    BONNIE
          That's nice.

                    STEVE
               (super excited)
          Open _your_ present, Jenny!

She tears her shoebox-shaped gift open: "Cowsurly Boots."

                    STEVE
          Don't worry they're the same as
          Cowgirly! GallMart, Savin'-some!

She looks to the shoebox: "Hot jingle-jangle-jingle action!"

                    STEVE
          I had to haggle some podunk lady
          terrorist for 'em but I won!

                    JENNY
          Good job, Papaw.

                    STEVE
          Try 'em on!

She kicks off her shoes then slides on the "Cowsurly Boots."

                    STEVE
          Do they fit?!

                    JENNY
          Yes.

                    STEVE
          Do a dance! Let's hear 'em!

She begrudgingly dances a pathetic jig--JINGLE-JANGLE-JINGLE.

                    ROBERT
               (wincing)
          They sure jingle-jangle-jingle.

                    STEVE
          Boy, they sure do!

                    LIZZY
               (still blubbering)
          Is everyone ready for the bonfire?

Robert pops another Xanadone.

EXT. BONFIRE IN THE WOODS - NIGHT

Near the BONFIRE, Bobby stands, constructing a s'mores before
a sitting Steve. Lizzy watches nearby eating her own s'mores.

                    BOBBY
          This is the only Christmas we're
          having this year, huh Papaw?

                    STEVE
          Yes, thank God.

                    BOBBY
          Why do you hate Christmas so much?

                    STEVE
          It brings back bad feelings.

                    BOBBY
          From what, Papaw?

                    STEVE
          Your Mamaw 'n I almost ruined
          Christmas a long time ago. We
          almost ruined our family. I guess
          Christmas just brings back the bad
          feelings from that year for us.

                    BOBBY
          What happened?

                    STEVE
          Your Dad 'n Aunt Lizzy saved
          Christmas 'n our family too.

                    BOBBY
          But what happened?

                    STEVE
          Mamaw 'n I split up.

                    BOBBY
          For real?

                    STEVE
          For real. The farm wasn't doing
          well 'n we had no money for Lizzy
          'n Rob's Christmas presents. Mamaw
          'n I got into a fight about it. We
          were gonna separate but Aunt Lizzy
          'n your Dad stopped that with their
          "Parent Trap Christmas." A pathetic
          attempt to get us back together. It
          worked, not their lovey-dovey date
          setups but the fact that they
          didn't care about getting Christmas
          presents 'n only wanted us back
          together. That's what really did
          it. Ya see, family is forever.

                    BOBBY
          But what about when you die?

                    STEVE
          After I die, you'll still remember
          the good times we had, Bobby.

Bobby hands Steve his s'mores. Lizzy wipes away a tear.

                    LIZZY
          Dad, can we talk?

                    STEVE
          Okay.

Steve takes a bite of the s'mores as he stands.

EXT. RED PARKED PICKUP IN THE WOODS - SECONDS LATER

Lizzy and Steve sit on the tailgate. Their feet dangle.

                    STEVE
          I hope you 'n Rob aren't too mad at
          me about the farm.

                    LIZZY
          Rob didn't even want it.

                    STEVE
          Did you want it?

                    LIZZY
               (erupting)
          Yes, why did you sell it, Dad?!

                    STEVE
          To keep a promise to your mother.

                    LIZZY
          Huh?

                    STEVE
          I had to break my promise of the
          farm to you in order to keep the
          promise I made to your mother.

                    LIZZY
          What promise did you make to Mom?

                    STEVE
          When I wanted to buy the farm,
          forty years ago, your mother would
          only let me buy it if I promised
          that I'd sell it one day 'n then
          with the sale-money we'd live out
          our golden years down in Florida.

                    LIZZY
          Really?

                    STEVE
          Yup, I already bought our condo
          down there at the Sunshine Towers.
          I'm sorry, Lizzy.

                    LIZZY
          I accept your apology.

                    STEVE
          You do?

                    LIZZY
          Yeah, Mom has dibs, dems da rules.
          Hey, let's go sing carols to
          Muhammad 'n Fatima like we used to.
          We won't get to ever again, Dad.

                    STEVE
               (smiling)
          Okay.

EXT. MUHAMMAD & FATIMA'S HOUSE - MOMENTS LATER

The entire Walton family stand before the front stoop,
lovingly singing "O Holy Night." Muhammad barges out.

                    MUHAMMAD
               (wild-eyed)
          Stop caroling, it's November!

They stop singing. Fatima appears in the doorway.

                    MUHAMMAD
          Are the terrorists making you all
          do this to push Christmas up and
          drive the American public insane?!

                    BONNIE
          What? No.

                    STEVE
          Yeah, it's just us, Muhammad.

                    MUHAMMAD
          Steve? You're alive?

                    STEVE
          Apparently.

                    MUHAMMAD
          Ya mean, you all are doing this on
          your own? You're the terrorists?

                    BONNIE
          I'm my own terrorist? Mind-blow.

Dave-O drives up in Lizzy's car. He and Gran jump out.

          DAVE-O   GRAN
     Surprise!   Surprise!

                    LIZZY
          Dave-O?

                    DAVE-O
          Everyone, this is my Gran!

Gran's kangaroo earrings swing as she puckers forth her
overly plump and glistening lips.

                    LIZZY
               (horrified)
          Gaw, trout-mouth.

                    GRAN
          Thanks for noticing, Lizzy! My
          husband, God rest, would never let
          me get 'em! He thought they'd look
          too fake! Shows him! I mean, what's
          more natch than a trout, 'ey?!

                    LIZZY
          Dave-O, why is your Gran here?

                    DAVE-O
          I got her from the airport.

                    LIZZY
          But why is she here?

                    DAVE-O
          All this family stuff over the past
          couple of days, made me realize I
          want her to be here for when I ask.

                    LIZZY
          For when you ask what?

Dave-O drops to one knee before her.

                    DAVE-O
          Will you marry me?

Jenny pulls out the small velvety box and flips it open to
reveal the gold-diamond-ring. It gleams.

                    BOBBY
          He's a stand-up bloke, Aunt Lizzy.

                    LIZZY
          Huh?

                    BOBBY
          Dave-O's a stand-up bloke, he told
          me about what "heavy pettin'"
          really means while y'all just let
          me keep saying it like an idiot.

              He's a stand-up bloke so say you'll
              marry him, Aunt Lizzy. Say, yes.

                        LIZZY
              Of course I'll marry him, yes!

Jenny hands the box to Dave-O who promptly removes the
gleaming gold-diamond-ring and slides it onto Lizzy's finger.

                        DAVE-O
              Does it, fit?

                        LIZZY
              Perfectly.

Dave-O stands. He and Lizzy kiss. Everyone claps.

                        DAVE-O
                   (excited and to Lizzy)
              I even bought the farm! I said it
              was taken care of, so, surprise!

                        LIZZY
                   (matching his excitement)
              We can have our wedding here next
              month, Dave-O! A Christmas wedding!

                        BOBBY
              Yay, two Christmases!

                        MUHAMMAD
              The FBI is coming! Look!

All look as SEVERAL FLASHING POLICE CARS approach them,
heading down the haphazardly paved country road.

                        BONNIE
              The FBI? Why?

                        MUHAMMAD
              I called 'em, I thought terrorists
              were holding you all hostage.

                        BONNIE
              Ya did?

                        MUHAMMAD
              I thought they were making you all
              force Christmas to come early.

                        BONNIE
              No, we decided to do that.

                    MUHAMMAD
          What about my tree?

                    BONNIE
          Lizzy got worked up into a tizzy
          again, craziest one yet. Sorry.

                    FATIMA
               (to Muhammad)
          I told you, Muhammad.

                    MUHAMMAD
               (to Bonnie)
          That's okay, I'll plant another.

                    FATIMA
          Wow, you're taking this well,
          habibi. Still can't wait to refill
          your mood stabilizers though.

                    MUHAMMAD
               (exploding)
          I told you a million times, Fatima,
          there's nothing wrong with my mood!

                    ROBERT
          Want a Xanadone, Muhammad?
               (rattling the bottle)
          Anybody? Xanadone?

All adults look to the still approaching FLASHING POLICE CARS
then look back to Robert. They jut their hands out, palms up.

                                        FADE OUT.